Moving Day

Moving Day

Anthony G. Brandon

Illustrated by Wong Herbert Yee

Green Light Readers
Harcourt, Inc.
Orlando Austin New York San Diego Toronto London

It was moving day.
Mr. and Mrs. Kim were moving.

Jenny Kim was moving.
Jack Kim was moving.

But not Annie.

"I'm not going," said Annie.
She sat on a box.

"Let's go," said Mrs. Kim.
"I'm not going," said Annie.

"You have to go," said Jenny.
"I'm not going," said Annie.

"We all have to go," said Jack.
"Well, I'm not going," said Annie.

"You will have a big yard," said Mrs. Kim.

"I like my little yard better!" said Annie.

"You will have a big room," said Mr. Kim.

"I like my little room better!" said Annie.

"You will make new friends," said Jenny.

"I like my old friends better," said Annie.

It was time to go.

"Annie, get the last box," said Mrs. Kim.
"Okay, but I'm still not going," said Annie.

"Is this puppy going?"

"Yes," they all said.
"Then I'm going, too!" said Annie.

Pack Your Suitcase

Pretend it is your moving day.
What special things will you pack?
Make a suitcase to carry them all!

construction paper

pipe cleaners

magazines

scissors

crayons

glue

hole punch

1 Fold the paper in half.

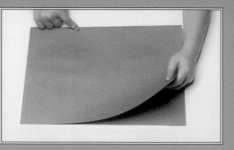

2 Make a handle for each side.

3 Fill your suitcase with pictures.

Ask a friend to guess what is in your suitcase. Then show and tell what you have inside!

Draw Your Dream House

What would your dream house be like? It can be big or small. It can be any color you want it to be. Maybe you would like to live there with your friends or family—or maybe you would like to live there all by yourself. You can build your dream house with your imagination!

markers,
colored pencils,
or crayons

 paper

1. Draw a picture of your dream house.

2. Write about your dream house.
Write why you would like to live there.

3. Share your dream
house with a
friend.

Meet the Illustrator

Wong Herbert Yee likes drawing animals—especially animals wearing clothes! The rabbit in *Moving Day* is special to him because it is his daughter's favorite stuffed animal. He likes to put that rabbit in every story he illustrates.

Wong Herbert Yee